Printed in Belgium
First U.S. edition, 2009

ISBN 978-1-59078-658-1

CIP data is available.

Lemniscaat
An Imprint of Boyds Mills Press, Inc.
815 Church Street
Honesdale, Pennsylvania 18431

Edward van de Vendel
& Martijn van der Linden

For You
and
No One Else

Lemniscaat
Honesdale, Pennsylvania

In the heart of the forest,
in a quiet spot,
Buck found a curiosity.

He sprang over white lilies and blue hyacinths, running quickly to Sparklehart.

"Sparkle!" he cried. "I have something curious for you! There was just one and I thought: this is for Sparklehart and no one else."

"Really?" said Sparklehart.
"Of course!" cried Buck. "Come with me and you can see it."

Buck and Sparklehart raced off together. Over thistle flowers and mossy turf they went until they were in the heart of the forest, at the quiet spot.

"Oh," said Sparklehart, "yes," and he plucked the curiosity
from the grass.

He counted the leaves. "You were right, Bucksey," he said.
"There are seven. It's a seven-leaf clover. How curious!"

"For you," said Buck, and he wanted to add "and no one else."

But Sparklehart had already run off. "Hey," he called, "come and look. There are more!"

How terrible! Further on, there were seven-leaf clovers everywhere.
Buck's gift wasn't curious. In fact, it wasn't special at all!

But Sparklehart bounded with all four legs right into the clover.
"Bucksey," he called joyfully, "you're my best friend. How lucky I am!"

He swooped his head down toward the ground and then back up again until he had filled his mouth with seven-leaf clovers.

Come on, he signaled, come on!

Off they went, side by side: Buck and Sparklehart. They flew over purple violets and yellow primroses until they were back.

Sparklehart dropped the clover and, panting, said, "This is going to be fantastic. Just watch!"

He strutted off among the trees. Buck followed, wondering where they were going. Soon he found out.

Sparklehart hurried toward Doe and offered her a seven-leaf clover. He said, "I have something curious for you. I found it in the forest. There was only one, and I thought: that's for Doe and no one else."

Buck wanted to say something to Sparklehart, but Sparklehart was already walking toward Doe Two. And then to Doe Three and Doe Four. He walked to Does Five and Six and Seven, to Does Eight, Nine, and Ten.

Buck heard Sparklehart say the same thing to each Doe: "I have something curious for you. There was only one, and I thought: This is for you and no one else."

Sparklehart walked back, laughing. "Hey, Bucksey! What are you waiting for? Now it's your turn. Here, I still have lots of clover left. Who are you going to give them to?"

Buck opened his mouth, but no words came out.
He shook his head and ran off.

Buck traveled over thornbushes and thick, twisting branches until he arrived at the heart of the forest, at a quiet spot. He dropped to the ground and laid his weary head in the grass.

A couple of hours later, he woke up and heard someone moving around. Sparklehart was watching him from a distance.

"Bucksey," said Sparklehart, "you disappeared! Do you know what happened? Three Does got really angry and made a fuss! Ha! Well, I'm glad I found you again. You were lying there trembling. Are you cold?"

"No ...," said Buck. "No ..."

But then he saw it. Right next to his hooves was a sprig of clo-
ver. He counted again and again. Twelve. A twelve-leaf clover.
And no, there weren't any others.
It was a curiosity.
A true curiosity.

At that moment, the sun began to shine brightly over the forest.
Buck began to feel better, but he was confused. Who was this clover for?
    Suddenly, the answer came to him. He plucked the twelve-leaf clover
from the grass. He stood up. He thrust the clover straight out in front of
him and said, "Sparkle, this is ... for you."

Sparklehart looked at Buck and at the twelve-leaf clover. He didn't say anything for a long time, and then he whispered, "For me? Really?"

Buck dropped the clover, and he shouted, right through the woods and flowers and paths and branches, louder than he had ever shouted before: